For Toby and Catherine – N.L.
For Laura – E.C.C.

Text copyright © Naomi Lewis 1999, 2014
Illustrations copyright © Emma Chichester Clark 1999, 2014
The rights of Naomi Lewis and Emma Chichester Clark to be identified
as the author and illustrator of this work have been asserted by them in
accordance with the Copyright, Designs and Patents Act, 1988 (United Kingdom).

First published in Great Britain in 1999 by Frances Lincoln Children's Books,
74-77 White Lion Street, London N1 9PF
www.franceslincoln.com

This edition published 2014

A catalogue record for this book is available from the British Library.

ISBN 978-1-84780-510-2

Printed in China

1 3 5 7 9 8 6 4 2

Tales from
HANS
CHRISTIAN
ANDERSEN

Naomi Lewis
Illustrated by Emma Chichester Clark

F
FRANCES LINCOLN
CHILDREN'S BOOKS

CONTENTS

INTRODUCTION

Genius must be the nearest thing to magic that any human being can possess. But what makes a genius? That's a hard question. Certainly, no one living in the stiff Danish town of Odense in the early years of the 19th century would have guessed that a penniless boy, "the washerwoman's crazy son", as he was called, would become one of the world's greatest storytellers.

Hans Christian Andersen (1805-1875) was the only child of very poor parents. His mother was an illiterate peasant woman. His father was very different: by trade a shoe-maker, he was a natural scholar and a rebel. He died when Hans Christian was only eleven, sure that his life had been a failure. But he was wrong: without knowing it, he left his son a gift that would mark his most original work. For when the boy was quite small, his father would take him into the woods and show him how even an insect or blade of grass had a character of its own. He made Hans Christian a toy theatre, where any tale could be acted out on a tiny scale. From this came that special feature of so many of Andersen's tales: things – not only toys, but any object lying around, a stick, a saucepan, a needle – can portray every kind of human feeling or behaviour.

The 14-year-old starveling scarecrow who made his way to Copenhagen saw himself initially as an actor, singer and dancer. Pleading, performing, knocking at doors of the famous, scholars, ministers, theatrical people, he attracted so much attention that the city virtually adopted him. An over-sensitive, overgrown, lonely boy, he had to endure a long, grim period of the education he had missed in his childhood. Then: choose your profession, Hans Christian, he was told. He chose to write. He began with grown-up novels, travel books, plays, but other things – strange little tales – kept rising up in his head. Soon, in translation, they were to make him known in England, America and throughout Europe.

The tales in this book all show Andersen at his exciting best. Several are well enough known and it's always a pleasure to meet them again. But two are extremely hard to find elsewhere: "Elf Hill" is an extraordinary story, funny and magical; and "Little Ida's Flowers" is like no other tale I have ever read. Another story which will be new to many children is the lively "Money Box Pig". Who else could have written it but Andersen? A special jewel is the last part of "The Nightingale" – one of the most marvellous scenes in the whole of fairy tale. But every tale has surprises, each time it is read.

Andersen wrote for all ages: you are never too young or too old to start. Once in your mind, his stories will last you a lifetime.

Naomi Lewis

THE PRINCESS AND THE PEA

There was once a prince who wanted to marry a princess but she had to be a real princess, and that was hard to find.

He travelled far and wide and met plenty of princesses, but not one of them seemed genuine. Something was always wrong, one thing or another, although he couldn't say exactly what it was. Finally he returned home, disappointed and sad, for he did so want to find a real princess.

One evening, there was a terrible storm. Thunder roared, lightning flashed, rain poured down in torrents. What a dreadful night to be outside without shelter! But someone *was* outside, for in the midst of the storm a knock was heard on the palace door. The old king himself went down to see who was there.

Standing at the door was a princess. But what a state she was in! The rain ran down her hair, through her clothes, into her shoes and out at the toes and heels.

Still, she *said* she was a real princess.

The old queen thought to herself, "Hmm, we'll soon find out if she is." She went into the spare bedroom, took all the bedclothes off the bed, and laid one small pea on the mattress. Then she piled twenty mattresses on top of the pea,

and twenty eiderdowns on top of the mattresses. And that was the princess's bed for the night.

Morning came.

"How did you sleep?" they asked her.

"Oh, not a wink the whole night long!" replied the princess. "I can't imagine what it was, but something has made me black and blue!"

So she *was* a real princess! Who else could have felt a pea through all those mattresses?

The prince's search was ended, and the two were married.

As for the pea, it was exhibited in the town museum. You can see it for yourself, if no one has taken it.

Now there's a fine story for you!

THE HAPPY FAMILY

Listen, and I'll tell you something: the biggest leaf of all the leaves in the country is the burdock leaf. A little girl could wear a single one as an apron. If she held it up by the stalk on a rainy day, she could use it as an umbrella. Burdocks never grow alone, so where you find one, you find plenty. They make a splendid show – but, when they were grown in days gone by, it was not for their looks, but as food, for snails! No, not ordinary snails, but special snails, large and white. Rich people used to have them made into a dinner dish called a fricassée. "Delicious!" they would murmur, as they ate. And that's why the burdocks were planted.

Now, there was once an old manor house surrounded by burdocks. No one living there ate snails – happily, the custom had died out years before, and the snails had gone, almost all of them. But the grounds were still full of burdock plants. They grew and grew; they spread all over the paths and flower beds – the garden was like a big forest. Here and there an apple or a plum tree rose up over the forest top; otherwise you would never have known that there was a garden beneath. And in the midst of all this green lived a pair of very old, large white snails, the last survivors of their kind.

How old were they? The snails themselves had no idea. But they did remember that once, in the past, they had not been alone.

Around them had lived many white-snail friends and relations. They knew, too, that their ancestors had come from distant lands, and that the whole vast burdock forest had been planted just for them. The old snails had never been outside: the forest was their world.

They also knew that there was something in the world called the Manor House. There you were "cooked", whatever that might mean: it seemed that you turned from white to black, and were laid on a Silver Dish – though what happened after that was a mystery. In any case, the snails could not imagine what it felt like to be "cooked" and laid on a Silver Dish, but they were sure it must be interesting. It was certainly grand and distinguished – no doubt about that. But what *did* happen afterwards? They could find out nothing. They asked other forest creatures – beetles, earthworms – but no one had any idea. It had certainly never happened to them.

The old snails were sure of one thing: they were the aristocrats of the forest world. It had been created for them, like the Manor House and the Silver Dish.

So they continued to live, day after day, in quiet happiness. As they had no children of their own, they adopted an ordinary little snail, and brought him up as their own. He never grew any bigger, for he was just a small common garden snail; but the parents, old Mother Snail especially, always thought that he had grown a bit since yesterday. And when Father Snail seemed unsure of this, she would ask him to feel the little shell. He would feel it, and agree that perhaps Mother Snail was right.

One day, there was a heavy shower of rain. "Just listen to the drum-drum-drum

on the leaves," said Father Snail. "Yes," said Mother Snail, "and look! Some of the drops are running right down the stalks. Everything on the ground will be soaked. How thankful I am for the good homes on our backs. We are so fortunate. Each of us has a house as soon as we are born. The burdock forest was planted just for us. Though I sometimes wonder just how far it goes, and what lies beyond."

"There is nothing beyond," said Father Snail. "Why should we look any further?"

"Oh, but I can't help wondering, now and then," said Mother Snail. "It would be so interesting to go to the Manor House and be 'cooked' – whatever that means – and laid on a Silver Dish. All our ancestors did, so it must be something fine."

"The Manor House may be in ruins by now," said Father Snail. "The burdocks must have grown right over it. But why are you so impatient? It is always rush, rush, rush with you, and now our little one is beginning to be the same. Why, in only three days he has nearly finished crawling up that stalk. It makes me quite giddy to watch him."

"Now, don't complain about our boy," said Mother Snail. "He crawls along

so carefully. He's going to be a great joy to us, I'm sure -and what more have we old folk to live for? But don't you think we should start to look for a wife for him? Don't you think that somewhere, deep in the forest, there might be a few of our own kind?"

"Well," said Father Snail, "I dare say there are plenty of slugs and such, without a house of their own. They fancy themselves, those creatures, but you surely wouldn't want us to stoop so low. Still, we might commission the ants to look around. They're always scurrying to and fro, as if they had plenty to do. They might know of a little wife for our son."

So that's what they did.

"Yes, yes," said the ants. "We know of a beautiful bride, but it might be hard to arrange. You see, she is a queen."

"Oh, that wouldn't matter," said Father Snail. "But has she a house?"

"She has a whole palace," said the ants. "It's an ant palace - most magnificent. It has seven hundred corridors!"

"Thank you," said Father Snail, "but our son is not going into an ant-hill. If that's the best you can do, we'll ask the gnats and the midges. They fly everywhere, rain or shine; they know every corner of the forest."

So that's what they did.

"Yes, indeed," said the gnats. "A hundred man-paces from here, on a gooseberry bush, is a little snail with a house of her own. She lives all by herself and is just old enough to get married."

"Very well," said Father Snail. "But she must make the journey. After all, our son has a whole burdock forest. She has only a bush."

So the gnats flew off to fetch the little snail-maiden. The journey took her over a

week, but that was as it should be. It showed that she came of a good snail family.

And so the wedding took place. Six glow-worms arranged the lighting. Otherwise it was a quiet affair, since the old snail-folk weren't used to merrymaking. Father Snail was too moved to speak. But Mother Snail made a charming speech. Then they handed over the whole of the burdock forest to the young couple, saying that it was the best place in the world. And if the young pair lived respectable lives, and had plenty of children, one day they and their family might be taken away to the Manor House and "cooked" – whatever that might mean – and laid in style on a Silver Dish.

When the ceremony was over, the two old snails retired into their houses and never came out again. There they slept, deeply and peacefully. The two young snails reigned long in the forest and had many children. But they were never brought to the Manor House, to be "cooked" and laid on a Silver Dish. So at last they decided that the old house had tumbled down, and that no more humans were left in the world.

Why should they think otherwise? The rain made music for them on the leaves: drum-a-drum-drum, drum-a-drum-drum. The sun shone, making the leaves dazzle their eyes with brightness. There never was a happier family in the world!

THE SHEPHERDESS
AND THE CHIMNEY-SWEEP

Have you ever seen a very old cupboard or cabinet, quite black with age, carved all over with trailing stems and leaves?

There was a cupboard of this kind in the room of our story. Once it had belonged to the children's great-great-grandmother. It was covered from top to bottom with carvings of roses and tulips, surrounded by curly flourishes, while, through the spaces, numbers of little carved deer poked out their antlered heads.

In the middle, though, there was something else: a being of sorts, a most peculiar character. It or he had legs like a goat, two small horns coming out of his forehead, a long beard and a rather sinister grin. The children of the house called him Grand-Master-Brigadier-Major-General-Captain-Sergeant-Corporal Goatlegs.

His eyes were turned all the time to the table under the mirror, for on it stood a lovely little china shepherdess. Her shoes were painted gold, her dress was neatly pinned with a china rose, she had a golden hat and in her hand was a shepherd's crook. Oh, she was beautiful!

Close behind her was a little chimney-sweep. He too was made of china.

All his clothes were black, but his face was as pink and white as a girl's. Really, he was only a make-believe sweep; the china-makers could just as easily have turned him out as a prince. There he stood, with his ladder and his pretty face, which hadn't a dab of soot on it. And since the sweep and the shepherdess had always been placed together on the table, they became engaged. Indeed, they were very well suited. Both were young; both were made of the same kind of china clay; each was as fine and fragile as the other.

Not far away was a very different figure, at least three times their size. This was an old Chinaman, a Mandarin who could nod his head. He too was made of china, and though he could supply no proof, he always declared that he was the shepherdess's grandfather. So when Major-General Goatlegs asked for her hand in marriage, the Mandarin nodded his consent.

"There's a fine husband for you," he said to the shepherdess. "He is made of real mahogany – I am almost sure of it – and you will become Madam-Lady-Grand-Master-Brigadier-Major-General-Captain-Sergeant-Corporal Goatlegs. He owns this whole cupboard full of silver plate, as well as what he has secretly hidden away."

"I don't want to go into that dark cupboard," said the little shepherdess. "I have heard that he has eleven china wives in there already."

"Then you can be the twelfth," said the Mandarin. "Tonight, as soon as the cupboard starts creaking, the wedding will take place, as sure as I'm a Chinaman!" With that, he nodded his head and went to sleep.

But the little shepherdess began to cry. She looked at her true love, the chimney-sweep. "I think I must ask you," she said, "to come out into the wide world with me, for we cannot stay here."

"Your will is my will," said the chimney-sweep. "Let us start out at once; I feel sure that I can earn enough to keep you by my profession."

"If only we could get down from the table," she said. "I cannot be happy until we are out in the wide world."

So the chimney-sweep comforted her, and told her where to place her foot on the carved projections and the gilded leaves of the table leg. He took his ladder to help her, and there they were at last on the floor. But when they looked up at the dark old cupboard – what a commotion! All the carved deer were poking out their heads even further, pricking their antlers and turning their necks from side to side. Brigadier-Major-General-Captain-Sergeant-Corporal Goatlegs was jumping up and down and shouting across to the old Chinaman, "They're running away! They're running away!"

Sure enough, when they reached the ground and looked back, they saw that the old Chinaman had woken and was rocking his body to and fro. He had to move like that, since, apart from his head, he was made all in one piece.

"The old Chinaman is coming!" shrieked the little shepherdess, and so terrified was she that she fell down on her porcelain knees.

"I have an idea," said the chimney-sweep. "Let us creep into the big pot-pourri jar over there in the corner. We can hide among the dried roses and lavender and throw salt in his eyes if he comes."

"That will not help," she said. "Besides, I happen to know that the old Chinaman and the pot-pourri jar were once engaged. No, there is nothing left for us but to go forth into the wide world."

The chimney-sweep gave her a keen and serious look. Then he said,

"The only path I know lies through the chimney. Are you sure you are brave enough to follow me through the heart of the stove and into the dark tunnel of the flue? That is the way to the chimney, and right at the top there is a hole that leads us into the wide world."

And he led her across to the door of the stove.

"It looks very black," she said. But she went with him all the same, through firebrick and flue, where the darkness was as black as night.

"Now we are in the chimney," he said. "And look! The loveliest star is shining over our heads!"

Yes, there was indeed a star in the sky, just overhead. It was shining down on them as though it wanted to show them the way. On they clambered,

on they crawled, up and up, up and up, higher and higher. It was a horrible journey! But the sweep kept lifting the shepherdess, showing her the best places for her to put her little china feet, until at last they arrived at the rim of the chimney-pot. There they sat down, tired out. And no wonder.

High above was the sky with all its stars. Down below was the town with all its roofs. They could see far, far around them, where the wide world lay. The shepherdess had never imagined anything like it. She laid her little head on the sweep's shoulder, and cried so bitterly that the gold was washed from her sash.

"Oh," she cried, "if only I were back again on the table under the mirror! I shall never be happy until I am there again. If you really care for me, I beg you to take me home."

The chimney-sweep gently reasoned with her. He reminded her of the Chinaman, and of Brigadier-Major-General Captain-Sergeant-Corporal Goatlegs. But she still wept with despair and kissed and clung to him, until he could not help agreeing to her wish.

So they crawled back down the chimney, and crept through the flue, and at last they found themselves back inside the dark cavern of the stove. They stood behind its door for a while, to hear what was going on in the room. Everything seemed quiet enough, so they peeped out.

But, oh! There in the middle of the floor lay the old Chinaman. Trying to run after them, he had fallen from his table, and now he lay broken into three pieces – his back, his front and his head, which had rolled into a corner. And Brigadier-Major-General-Captain-Sergeant-Corporal Goatlegs? He stood where he had always stood. He looked deep in thought.

"How terrible!" cried the little shepherdess. "Old grandfather is broken into bits, and it is all our fault." She wrung her little hands.

"He can be mended," said the chimney-sweep. "Now don't get so excited. When they have glued him together and put a rivet in his neck, he'll be as good as new. He'll be able to say plenty of tiresome things to us yet."

"Well, if you think so," she said. And they climbed back to the table-top, where they had always stood.

"We *have* been a long way," said the chimney-sweep, "and here we are, back where we started. We might have spared ourselves the journey."

"Oh, if only old grandfather were mended," said the shepherdess. "Will it cost very much, do you think?"

The Chinaman was mended. The family had his back and front glued together. A rivet was put in his neck, and he looked as good as new. But he could no longer nod his head.

"You have become high and mighty since you were broken!" said Brigadier-Major-General-Captain-Sergeant-Corporal Goatlegs. "But what are you so proud of? Tell me – am I to have the shepherdess or not?"

The sweep and the shepherdess looked anxiously at the old Chinaman, for they were afraid that he might nod. But now he could not do this, and he did not wish to admit that he had a rivet in his neck. So the little porcelain lovers stayed together, and loved each other in the greatest happiness until they broke.

THE MONEY BOX PIG

In the children's playroom, toys lay everywhere. Only the money box pig had a place of his own; he stood by himself on the top of the cupboard. He was made of earthenware, with a slit in his back. Someone had made the slit larger with a knife, so that big silver coins could go in. There were two of these inside him already, as well as plenty of coppers. Indeed, he was crammed so full that he couldn't rattle. And if you are a money box pig, you can't rise higher in the world than that. There he stood, looking down on all the toys below. He knew very well that what he had inside him could buy the whole room and everything in it. All the toys knew this too, though they kept their thoughts to themselves.

In the chest-of-drawers one drawer was half open, and a big doll, who had been left inside, peered over the top. She was quite old. Her neck had been mended with a rivet.

She called out, "Let's play Humans. That's always good fun!" This caused quite a commotion; the toys grew rather excited. Even the pictures on the wall turned round to show their backs, but that was only high spirits.

By now it was midnight. The moon shone through the window, so they had free lighting. Everyone was invited to join in the game – even the pram, which didn't really belong. The only one to receive a written invitation was the money box pig. The dolls were afraid that he was too high up to hear a spoken message. Anyhow, he didn't answer. If he was to take part, it must be from his own place. They understood this, and got on with the arrangements.

They placed the little toy theatre in such a way that the money box pig could look right into it. They meant to begin with a play; then there would be tea and what they called "serious conversation". But somehow they began with the talk straight away. The rocking-horse spoke about racing stables and pedigrees; the pram went on about railways and steam power. Each one kept to his own line of business. The clock on the wall gave pronounced views on politics – tick, tick, tick. Time was in his hands, he declared. He alone could tell you when. But the dolls always said that he was hardly ever right – more often he was slow. The walking stick stood in an elegant pose. He liked to show off his silver knob on top and the brass ferrule at his other end.

The two embroidered cushions on the sofa lay there simpering. They were just pretty and silly.

At last it was time for the play. The audience was told that any noise could be made to show applause – banging, clapping, cheering, whistling, thumping on the floor. The riding whip declared that he would "crack" for the young ones not yet courting or engaged, but not for the old ones – they were so boring.

"Oh, I'll crack for anyone," said the firecracker.

The play was what you'd call so-so – there was not much of a plot – but the acting was excellent. All the cast presented their painted sides to the audience; they weren't meant to be seen on the other. They stood at the very front of the stage (they had to, because their strings were too long), but that made them easier to see. The doll in the drawer – the one with the mended neck – was so thrilled that she almost lost her head again. The money box pig was excited too, though he didn't show it. He began to think he might leave one of the performers something in his will. He might even let him share his funeral, when the time came.

They all enjoyed the play so much that they decided to miss tea and have more "serious conversation". That made them feel they were really playing at Humans! In fact, they were more like humans than they knew: each one secretly thought that his own opinions were more important than anyone else's; and all of them wondered what the money box pig was thinking.

The money box pig was still thinking about his will and his funeral, when – crash! he toppled over the cupboard's edge, and lay smashed into pieces on the floor. As for the coins, they went hopping, skipping or rolling about. The small ones circled around. The two big silver coins trundled off more solemnly, one in particular that longed to be out in the world. And out in the world it was, willy nilly; so were they all.

The broken bits of the money box pig were swept up and dropped in the dustbin. Next day, what's more, there on the cupboard top stood a new money box pig. It hadn't a single coin inside it yet, so it didn't rattle; that was one thing it shared with the other. It was just at the start of its story – and that makes a good place to end our own.

THE LITTLE MATCH GIRL

It was terribly cold. Snow was falling; soon it would be night. This was the very last evening of the year – New Year's Eve – and through the cold and darkness a poor little girl was wandering, barefoot and bareheaded. True, she had slippers when she started out from home, but where were they now? They were great big things, those slippers; once they had been her mother's. No wonder they had fallen off when she was hurrying across the road, just between two carriages that were thundering past. One slipper she couldn't find at all. As for the other, a boy had run off with it. It was big enough, he shouted, to do for a cradle one day, when he had children of his own.

So the little girl wandered on. Her feet were blue with cold. In an old apron she carried a pile of matches, tied in bundles. One of these bundles she held out in her free hand. But all through the day she had had no luck. No one had bought from her. No one had given her a single penny. Hungry and frozen, she drifted along. How miserable she looked! Yet she was pretty enough. The snowflakes fell on her pale fair hair, which curled about her neck.

But she certainly was not thinking of how she looked. Her thoughts were on the lights in all the windows, and the wonderful smell of roast goose dinners that floated down the street. Remember, it was New Year's Eve.

She found a sheltered corner made by two house walls, one house built further forward than the other. There she crouched down, huddling herself together, tucking up her legs. But it made no difference. She just grew colder and colder. What was the use of going home? She hadn't a single coin to take back with her, so her father would certainly beat her. Besides, her home was freezing too. It was just an attic under the roof; the wind whistled through the cracks, even though the worst of them had been stuffed with rags and straw.

How cold and numb her hands felt! A lighted match – now, what a comfort that would be. Oh, if only she dared to strike a single one – just one. She took a match and struck it against the wall – crrritch! How it crackled and blazed! What a lovely clear flame! It was just like a little candle. She held her hand around it. The match gave out a wonderful light. She started to dream: she was sitting in front of a big iron stove with shining brass knobs and fittings. Inside was a big friendly fire. But just as she had put her feet towards the warmth, the flame went out. Where was the stove? She was back again in the cold, with a burnt-out matchstick in her hand.

She struck another match. It flared up brightly, and where it shone the wall seemed transparent, like gauze. She could see right into a room where the table was covered with a white starched cloth. On it were dishes of the finest porcelain china. A delicious smell rose from a roast goose stuffed with prunes and apples. The goose seemed nearer and nearer; she could almost touch it. Then the match went out. All she could see and feel was the bleak, unfriendly wall.

She struck another match. Now she was sitting under the loveliest of Christmas trees. It was even bigger and more splendidly decorated than the great tree she had seen through the glass doors of the rich merchant's shop down the street. Thousands of candles were alight on its branches. Bright coloured pictures, like the ones in all the shop windows, gazed down on her kindly.

The little girl reached out her hands – then the match burnt out. But – how strange! The flames from the candles seemed to rise higher and higher. Why? She looked up. She was outside, but light came from the stars in the heavens high above. One star rushed across, leaving a fiery streak in the dark night sky.

"Someone is dying," said the little girl to herself. Her grandmother had told her once that whenever a star is in flight, it means that a soul is going to heaven. She was dead now, her old grandmother, the only person who had ever been kind to her.

She struck another match on the wall. As it shone out in the darkness, she saw her dear grandmother in the glow. How loving and kind she looked!

"Oh Granny, take me with you!" cried the little girl. "I know you'll disappear

when the match goes out, just like the warm stove and the roast goose and the wonderful tree." And as fast as she could, she struck all the rest of the matches in the bundle. Grandmother must not go.

The matches made such a brilliant light that all around seemed brighter than day. Never before had her Granny looked so tall and beautiful! She took the little girl in her arms and flew with her, up and up to where there was no cold, no fear, no hunger, up to heaven.

In the chill early morning, huddled in a corner, there sat the little match girl, frozen to death on the last night of the year.

Yet she seemed to be smiling.

As the New Year dawned on the small dead body with its lapful of matches, people saw that one bundle was burnt out. "She was trying to warm herself," they said. No one knew what lovely things she had seen, and how gloriously she had flown with her grandmother into her own New Year.

ELF HILL

Some lizards were scuttling about in the cracks of a tree. "I say, what a rumbling and tumbling is going on in Elf Hill," declared one. "The noise! I haven't slept a wink these last two nights."

"Oh, something is going on there, that's for sure," said another. "Last night the hill was raised on four pillars – they glowed like fire. Right up until cockcrow, too. It has certainly had a real airing. And the young elf-girls are learning new dances with plenty of stamping in them – thump, thump, thump. Mark my words, there's something afoot down there."

"I've had a chat with an earthworm I happen to know," said a third lizard. "He was just coming out of the Hill and he'd heard a great deal. Of course, he can't see, poor fellow, but for listening he's hard to beat. He says that the elves are expecting important visitors. The will-o'-the-wisps have been called in to help. They are to make a torchlight procession."

"Who can these visitors be?" the lizards asked each other.

At that moment Elf Hill opened, and out tripped an old elf-woman. She was the Elf-King's housekeeper. Goodness, she was quick on her toes! Trip, trip, she was off to the marsh to see the night-raven.

"You are invited to Elf Hill tonight," she told the bird. "But first you must do me a favour, and deliver the invitations. We're having some very distinguished guests, trolls of the highest quality; our Elf-King wants to impress them."

"Who shall I invite?" asked the raven.

"Well, anyone may come to the grand ball – even humans, so long as they can talk in their sleep or have other gifts of the elfin kind. But for tonight's banquet, the guests have been very carefully chosen. I've been arguing with the king about this. In my opinion, even ghosts shouldn't be asked. The first invitation should go to the Mer-King and his mermaid daughters. They are not very keen on coming ashore, I know, so tell them that they can count on having at least a wet stone each. I fancy they won't refuse. All the high-ranking trolls with tails must be asked, as well as the river-sprite and the goblins. Then there's the graveyard pig, the hell-horse and the church lamb – it wouldn't do to forget them."

"Caw!" croaked the night-raven, and he flew off to do the inviting.

The young elf-girls were already dancing on the hill. Floating around them were shawls woven of mist and moonshine – very pretty, if you like that sort of thing.

The great hall in the centre of the hill had been thoroughly cleaned. The walls shone like tulip petals with the light behind them. The Elf-King's golden crown had been polished up with ground slate pencils – but only pencils used by the cleverest scholars. Everyone rushed about – oh, the hurrying and scurrying!

"Now we must burn some horsehair and pig's bristles, to make a delicious smell," said the old housekeeper. "Then I've done my share."

"Please, dearest Daddy," begged the youngest of the Elf-King's daughters, "won't you tell us who these distinguished guests are?"

"Well, I suppose I must," said the king. "Two of you girls must be prepared to get married. The Great Troll of Norway is coming with his two boys – they are all three looking for wives. The old one owns a number of granite castles and a goldmine or two, so that's not bad. He's a good chum of mine – a real down-to-earth Norwegian. He came down here to fetch his first wife, but she's been dead a long while now. They do say that his sons are a pair of spoilt young brats – no manners at all. But they'll improve with time – you girls will just have to keep them in order!"

At that moment two will-o'-the-wisps flitted in.

"They're coming! They're coming!" they cried together.

"Hand me my crown. I shall go out and stand in the moonlight," said the Elf-King, and he went to meet his guests. His daughters followed, curtseying low to the ground.

And there he was – the Great Troll, with his crown of icicles and polished fir cones, his bearskin and sleigh boots. But his two teenage boys were lightly dressed – they were tough young fellows.

"Call this a hill?" said one, pointing his thumb at the Elf Hill. "In Norway we would call this a hole."

"Now then, boys," said the old troll. "Holes go downwards, hills go upwards. Don't you have eyes in your heads? You'd better behave yourselves, or everyone will think you are daft."

They entered the great hall, where all the special guests had assembled. The Mer-King and his mermaid daughters sat in tubs full of water; they felt quite at home, they said. Everyone was on best behaviour – with two exceptions: those Norwegian teenage trolls.

They started by putting their feet on the table.

"Take your feet out of the dishes!" shouted their father.

They obeyed, but took their time over it. Then they tickled their dinner partners – two elf-ladies – with pine cones. After that, they pulled off their boots to be more comfortable.

But the old troll was entirely different. He began to tell wonderful tales of the great Norwegian mountains and rushing waterfalls that sped down the cliffs with a sound like thunder. He spoke of the salmon that leapt in the racing torrent, while the water-sprite played its golden harp. He told of glittering winter nights, when the air was filled with jingling sleigh bells, and the young folk, carrying blazing torches, skated over the shining ice, which was so clear, so transparent that you could see the fishes fleeing in fear below.

Suddenly he stopped, and gave an elderly elfin lady a smacking kiss. They were complete strangers – but did that matter?

Now it was time for the elf-girls' display. They began with quite a simple dance, then changed to the stamping beat that they had been practising – what a treat! They ended with a strange free-style performance called "Breaking the Rules". Goodness, what twirling and twisting! Just watching it made you giddy. The hell-horse felt quite faint and had to leave the table.

"Whew!" said the old troll. "That was something! But can they do anything else?"

"They certainly can – as you shall see," said the Elf-King.

He called for his youngest daughter. She was small and slight, fair as moonshine – the most delicate of the sisters. She put a white sliver of wood in her mouth – and vanished! That was her special gift.

"Hmmm," said the old troll. He didn't want a wife with that particular trick.

The second sister could walk beside herself, so that she seemed to have a shadow. As you know, trolls and elves don't go in for shadows.

The third was a very different character. Besides being a fine brewer of beer, she knew how to decorate alder-stumps with glow-worms.

"She'd make a good housewife," said the old troll.

Now it was the fourth sister's turn. She was a harp player. When she plucked the first string, they all lifted their left leg. When she plucked the second string, they all had to do what she told them.

"She's a dangerous woman!" said the old troll. "What can the next one do?"

"I have heard so much about Norway," said the fifth elf-daughter, "that the only husband I will ever have must be Norwegian."

But the youngest sister whispered to the troll, "She says that only because she once heard a Norwegian folk song which said that, when the world ends, only the great hills of Norway will remain. She's afraid of the last day."

"Aha!" said the old troll. "So that's what it's all about. And the next?"

But the sixth girl held back. "I can only tell people the truth," she said, "and no one wants to hear that. So I spend my time sewing my shroud."

Now came the seventh and last of the daughters. She could tell stories – as many as you wished to hear.

"See my five fingers?" said the troll. "Tell me a tale for each."

The elf-girl took his hand in hers and began. The story made him laugh out loud. Presently she came to the ring finger; it had a gold band round it. "Stop!" the old troll called out. "Hold on to that finger. My hand is yours. You're the wife for me."

But the elf-girl said that she hadn't finished. There were still two more fingers. "They can wait," said the old troll. "We'll hear those tales in the winter. And you can tell me about the trees, and the wood spirits bringing their gifts, and the glittering, crackling frost. We'll sit in my granite hall, lit in blazing pine chips, and drink mead out of golden drinking horns that belonged to ancient Viking kings. Oh, we'll have a glorious time. The salmon will leap against our good stone walls, but we won't let them in. Now where are those boys?"

Where indeed? They were rushing around the fields blowing out the will-o'-the-wisps, who were preparing their torchlight procession.

"What disgraceful behaviour!" thundered their father. "I have chosen a mother for you. Now you can find wives for yourselves among her sisters."

But the lads replied that marriage wasn't for them. They took off their jackets and lay down on the table to sleep; they didn't care what they did.

Then the old troll danced over the hill with his young bride, and exchanged boots with her. That's far more elegant than exchanging rings.

"The cock's crowing!" cried the young elf-housekeeper. "We'll have to work fast and close the shutters, or the sun will burn us up."

So Elf Hill closed until night. But outside in the daylight, the lizards were still darting about in the ancient tree.

"Oh, I did like that old troll," said one.

"I liked the boys best," said the earthworm.

But then – the poor silly creature couldn't see.

LITTLE IDA'S FLOWERS

"Oh, my poor flowers – they look quite dead," said little Ida. "Last evening they were so fresh and lovely. What do you think has happened?"

She was asking the student, who was sitting, as usual, on the sofa. Ida was very fond of him. He knew the most surprising stories, and with his scissors he could cut wonders out of paper – hearts with tiny ballerinas inside, flowers, witches, castles with doors that opened.

"Don't you know?" said the student. "All last night they were dancing, and now they are tired out."

"But flowers can't dance," said little Ida.

"Oh, can't they!" said the student. "When night comes, and the human people are in bed asleep, the dancing starts. They have parties almost every night. You've seen the king's summer palace, with its beautiful gardens, just outside the town? There are magnificent dances in those gardens, I can tell you."

"I was there yesterday, with Mama," said little Ida, "but there wasn't a single flower. There were so many in the summer. What became of them?"

"I'll tell you," said the student. "When summer ends, and the king and queen and all the court go back to the city, the flowers move into the castle. They have a glorious time! The two finest roses take the throne; they are the king and queen. Tall tiger-lilies line up on either side; they are lords-in-waiting. Then all the most beautiful flowers glide in, and the grand ball begins. The dark blue violets are young naval cadets; they dance with the hyacinths and crocuses, and call them 'Miss'. They have to be polite in front of the tulips and big yellow lilies; those are the grown-ups in charge, who see that everyone behaves and dances properly."

"But tell me," said little Ida, "does the king allow the flowers to dance in his castle?"

"Nobody human is supposed to know about the goings-on," said the student. "You'd think the old steward might notice something when he makes his nightly rounds. But as soon as the flowers hear the jingle of his great bunch of keys, they hide behind the long curtains, peeping out now and then, the saucy things. 'Hmmm ... I seem to get a whiff of flowers from somewhere,' the old fellow mumbles, 'but there's not a leaf to be seen.'"

"Oh, I like that," said little Ida, clapping her hands. "You do make me laugh." Indeed, she could hardly stop laughing as she spoke.

"Preposterous! Nonsense! Fancy filling a child's head with such rubbish!" said the grumpy old councillor, who had just looked in and settled himself on the sofa. He could not abide the student, and was particularly cross when he saw him cutting out his fantastical paper figures. "What rubbish to put into a child's mind."

But little Ida enjoyed the student's stories, and she thought for a long time about his news of the flowers. So they drooped because they were tired out from dancing all night! They were certainly very weak. She took them along to the little table where she had arranged some of her toys. One was her doll Sophie,

comfortably asleep in her own special bed. But Ida said to her, "You will have to get up, Sophie. You mustn't mind sleeping in the table drawer tonight. My poor flowers are ill. I'm putting them in your bed."

Sophie didn't answer. She looked really cross as Ida picked her up. Still, you can't blame her for that.

When Ida had put her in the drawer, she laid the flowers in the bed and tucked them in. Surely they would be well again in the morning!

Presently it was time for Ida to go to bed. But first she peeped behind the window curtains, where her mother's hyacinths and tulips were arranged along the sill. She whispered to them softly, "I know where you're going tonight." The flowers never stirred a leaf, but Ida knew very well what they were planning.

She went to bed, but lay awake for a long time. One thought filled her mind: how exciting it would be to see the flowers dancing at the palace! She wondered if her own flowers would join them. At last she fell asleep, but even then, her dreams were about the flowers, and the councillor, and the student and his stories.

At midnight, she woke up. There wasn't a sound in the bedroom.

"I wonder if my flowers are still in Sophie's bed," she said to herself. "I would like to know."

She sat up and looked through the open door. Then – she did hear a sound: in the other room a piano was being played, very softly, and the music seemed to her more beautiful than any she had ever heard before.

"The flowers must all be dancing in there," she thought. "Oh, I *would* like to see them." The music was so thrilling that she couldn't wait any longer. She crept out and peeped into the other room.

What a lovely sight! The moon was shining through the window. It was almost as bright as daylight. Her mother's hyacinths and tulips stood in two long rows; Ida looked to see if any were left on the windowsill. There were none: every pot was empty. All the flowers were doing an elegant dance, holding each other's leaves. They formed chains and swung around. It was wonderful to watch.

Nobody noticed Ida, but she saw a deep blue crocus spring onto the table with the toys, and go straight to Sophie's bed. He pulled the curtains aside, and there were the flowers. Strange! They looked quite lively, not at all ill. Nothing would stop them now from joining the dance. The china chimney-sweep with a broken lip was the first to welcome them, with a bow, but they were far too excited to notice.

Suddenly, something fell from the table. Thump!

It was the toy that Ida had been given at the Easter Carnival – a bunch of twigs, really, tied with ribbons and topped with paper streamers. This twig-toy promptly began to dance the mazurka all by himself. The flowers' fragile stems couldn't manage the stamping part, but the twigs did it perfectly.

At last the music stopped for a moment, and in the pause a loud knock sounded from the table drawer where Sophie had been left for the night. The chimney-sweep ran bravely along the edge of the table, lay at full length, face downwards, and managed to push the drawer open.

Sophie sat up and put out her head. "There's a dance going on!" she exclaimed. "Why didn't anyone tell me?"

"Would you care to dance with me?" asked the china sweep.

"I should think not!" said the rude doll. "Besides, your face is chipped." She sat down on the edge of the drawer, waiting for one of the flowers to ask her to dance, but none of them did. She kept on making noises like "Ahem! Ahem!"

Still nobody noticed her. Even the sweep went off and danced by himself, and he didn't dance badly, either.

So, tired of being neglected, Sophie arranged to fall down on the floor. Thud! Everyone heard *this* noise. All the flowers came running over, full of concern.

"Are you hurt?" they asked. How kindly they behaved! And Ida's flowers thanked her for the lovely bed she had lent them.

They took Sophie to the brightest patch of moonlight in the middle of the room and danced with her, while the other flowers made a circle around them. Sophie was so pleased with all this attention that she told them, "You may keep the bed." She didn't really mean it, though.

But the flowers answered, "Thank you so much, but we don't live long. Indeed, we have only until tomorrow; then we'll be gone. But please tell little Ida to bury us in the garden where the canary was buried. Then next year we shall spring up again, green and new, and even prettier than before."

"No, no, you mustn't die," said Sophie, and she hugged the flowers.

Just then the door opened, and a whole crowd of lovely flowers came dancing in. Ida wondered where they came from. Can you guess? They came from the king's palace.

Two splendid roses, wearing golden crowns, led the way. They were the flower king and queen. Next came the sweet-scented stocks and carnations, bowing to left and right. They had brought their own music too – a band of poppies and peonies blowing on tiny sweet-pea pods. They blew so hard that their scarlet petals almost turned purple. After these, a host of other flowers glided in – violets, daisies, lilies-of-the-valley, weaving in and out in a dance of their own.

But everything must come to an end, and at last the ball was over. There was plenty of kissing and saying goodbyes, as the dancers floated away into the dawn. No one had seen little Ida. She crept away to her own bed, but in her dreams she lived again through the sights and sounds of that wonderful night.

Next morning she hurried to the table to see if the flowers were back in Sophie's bed. Yes, they were there, but they looked worn out, with shrivelled leaves.

There was not a spark of life in them. What about Sophie? She was in the drawer all right, just where Ida had put her. She looked extremely sleepy.

"Can you remember the message you were supposed to tell me?" asked Ida.

But Sophie's face stayed dull and stupid. She didn't answer.

"You are very naughty," said Ida. "The flowers danced with you too, and they were so kind and thoughtful."

She took a small cardboard box with a picture of a bird on the lid, and placed the flowers inside. "Now you have a nice coffin," she told them. "When my Norwegian cousins come, they will help me to bury you in the garden. Then you can live again in the summer and look even lovelier than before."

Ida's Norwegian cousins were two lively boys called Jonas and Adolph. Their father had just given them bows and arrows, and they brought them to show to Ida.

She told them about the flowers, and they planned a funeral. The boys walked ahead with their bows over their shoulders, and Ida followed them with the box.

In a corner of the garden they dug a little grave, where Ida laid the flowers in their box.

"Farewell, flowers – until next year!" said Ida.

And since the boys had no guns to fire, they each shot an arrow over the grave.

THE JUMPING COMPETITION

Three great jumpers – the Flea, the Grasshopper, and the Jumping Jack – held a jumping match to decide which of them was the best. They invited all the world, and anyone else who cared to come. All three looked like champions, as they waited for the competition to start.

"Well," said the king, "honour is a fine thing – but we also need a handsome reward. My daughter shall be wife to the winner!"

The first competitor to step forward was the Flea. He had fine manners and made elegant bows to the right and left – but then, he did have the blood of well-bred young maidens in him; indeed, he was always mixing with humans of quality.

Next came the Grasshopper. He was much larger than the Flea. He moved gracefully and with style, wearing a bright green uniform – the same uniform he had worn since he was born. He claimed not only to have ancient family connections with Egypt, but also that he was highly respected in modern Denmark, where this tale belongs. "When I was first brought in from the fields," he said, "I was given a special little house to live in, made from playing cards – only Kings and Queens, naturally." Then he boasted about his voice. "I sing so well," he declared,

"that sixteen crickets have fretted themselves into shadows hearing me sing."

On and on the two insects went, giving glowing accounts of themselves. Each wanted to be the husband of a princess.

Now we come to the third, the Jumping Jack. He was made from a goose's wishbone, two rubber bands, a little wooden stick and a blob of sealing wax. He said nothing at all, so everyone said he must be a deep thinker. The palace dog sniffed at him – sniff, sniff – so everyone said he must come from high-class stock. As for the old councillor, he said that the Jumping Jack could foretell the future: you could tell from his wishbone whether the winter would be mild or hard – and you couldn't tell *that* from looking at a weather forecaster!

"I shall not try to guess the winner," said the old king, "I prefer to keep my thoughts to myself."

The competition began.

The Flea jumped so high that he seemed to disappear – no one could see where he landed. In fact, some crows who were watching declared that he hadn't really jumped!

The Grasshopper jumped only half as high; but he landed in the old king's face. "Disgusting behaviour!" said the king. And that was the end for him.

As for the Jumping Jack, he sat so long without moving that people began to worry. What was he thinking? Was he planning his move? Or was it that he couldn't jump at all?

"I hope he isn't feeling ill," said the palace dog, and he went over to sniff the Jumping Jack again. But this time, his nose gave it a push. *Crick! Whirrrr!* Then Jumping Jack gave a little leap sideways, and landed – where do you think? –

right in the lap of the young princess, who was sitting on a little golden stool.

The king announced, "The highest jump of all was the jump onto my royal daughter. It needed a good head as well as good legs. The Jumping Jack has both."

And so the Jumping Jack won the princess.

"My jump was the highest," said the Flea afterwards. "But what do I care? She can have the old wishbone, stick and wax and all. I know I'm the real winner, but in this world you need more than skill and quality to win." He went off, joined the army, and they say he died in battle. Maybe yes, maybe no. So much for the Flea.

The Grasshopper sat down in a ditch to think about the ways of the world. "To get anywhere in life," he reflected, "you need influence. You need publicity." And he sang his own sad song, and that's how we heard this story.

But just because you read it here, that doesn't mean it's true.

THE NIGHTINGALE

This tale of ancient China happened many years ago, but that's exactly why you should hear it now, before it is forgotten.

The Chinese Emperor's palace was the finest in the world. It was made of the rarest porcelain, so fragile and delicate that you had to take the greatest care when you moved about. The palace garden was full of marvellous flowers; the loveliest of all had little silver bells tied to them – tinkle, tinkle, tinkle – to make sure that nobody passed without noticing them.

Yes, everything in the Emperor's garden was wonderfully planned, and it stretched so far that even the gardener had no idea where it ended. If you kept on walking, you found yourself in a most beautiful forest with towering trees and very deep lakes. This forest went right down to the sea.

In the high branches of the trees, there lived a nightingale. She sang so sweetly that even the poor fisherman, working nearby, would stop while casting his nets each night, to listen. "Ah, it's a treat to hear," he would say.

From every country in the world, travellers came to admire the Emperor's city, his palace and his garden. But as soon as they heard the nightingale, they would declare, "Now that's the best thing of all." Learned men wrote books about the city and the palace and the great garden, but they praised the nightingale above all other marvels, and poets wrote thrilling poems about the bird in the forest near the sea.

These books were read all over the world, and one day some of them reached the Emperor. There he sat in his golden chair, reading descriptions of his realm. Suddenly he came to the sentence: "But, with all these wonders, nothing can match the song of the nightingale."

"What's this?" said the Emperor. "The nightingale? Why, I've never heard of it. Just imagine! The things one learns from books!"

He sent for his lord-in-waiting. "I see in this book that we have a most remarkable bird called a nightingale," said the Emperor. "It's supposed to be the finest thing in my vast empire. Why has no one ever told me about it?"

"Well," said the lord-in-waiting, "I have never heard anyone mention the creature. Certainly, it has never been presented at court."

"It is my wish that it comes here tonight and sings to me," said the Emperor.

"*Tsing-pe!*" said the lord-in-waiting, and he ran up and down all the stairs and through all the halls and passages. Half the court ran with him.

At last they came across a poor little girl in the kitchen. "The nightingale?" she said. "Yes, of course I know it. How that bird can sing! Most evenings, after work, they let me take home a few left-over scraps for my sick mother – she lives by the lake at the other side of the wood. And when I am on my way back, and feeling tired, I sit down for a while and listen. Then I hear the nightingale."

"Little kitchen-girl," said the lord-in-waiting, "I guarantee you a permanent kitchen appointment and permission to watch the Emperor dining, if only you will lead us to the nightingale."

So the courtiers set out for the forest. As they trailed along, a cow began to moo.

"Oh!" exclaimed a page. "Now we can hear it! For such a small creature it makes a wonderfully powerful noise!"

"No, no, that's a cow mooing," said the little kitchen-maid.

Some frogs began croaking in the pond. "Glorious, glorious!" said the Emperor's chaplain. "It's just like tiny church bells!"

"No, those are frogs," said the kitchen-maid. "I think we'll hear her any minute now."

Then the nightingale began to sing. "There she is!" said the girl. "Look!" And she pointed to a little grey bird up among the branches.

"Little nightingale!" called the kitchen-maid. "Our gracious Emperor would very much like you to sing for him."

"With the greatest of pleasure," said the nightingale, and she sang so beautifully that it was a delight to hear.

"Shall I sing once again for the Emperor?" asked the nightingale. She thought that the Emperor was one of these visitors.

"Most excellent nightingale!" said the lord-in-waiting. "I have the honour and pleasure to summon you to a concert this evening at the palace, where you may enchant His Imperial Majesty with your delightful song."

"My song sounds best out in the forest," said the nightingale. Still, she went along willingly enough.

Meanwhile, what a cleaning and polishing were going on at the palace! Right in the middle of the great hall, a golden perch was set up. This was for the nightingale. Everyone in the court was there; even the little kitchen maid was allowed to stand behind the door. All eyes were turned on the little grey bird as the Emperor nodded at her to begin.

Then the nightingale sang so beautifully that tears came into the Emperor's eyes, and rolled down his cheeks. She sang on even more thrillingly, and every note went straight to his heart. The nightingale, he declared, should have his golden slipper to wear around her neck. But she thanked him and refused. "Can any gift be greater than an Emperor's tears?" she said. "I have had pay enough." And she sang yet another song in her ravishing voice.

She was now to live at court, in her own cage, with permission to take the air twice in the daytime and once each night. With her on each excursion went twelve attendants, each one holding firmly on to a silk ribbon tied to the bird's leg. There was not much fun in those outings!

One day, a large parcel arrived for the Emperor. On it was written one word: NIGHTINGALE.

"Why, here's a new book about our famous bird!" said the Emperor. But it wasn't a book; it was a little mechanical toy in a box - a clockwork nightingale.

It was made to look like the real one, but it was covered all over with diamonds, rubies and sapphires. If you wound it up, it would sing one of the songs that the real bird sang, and its tail would go up and down, glittering with silver and gold. Round its neck hung a ribbon on which were the words, "The Emperor of Japan's nightingale is a poor thing beside the nightingale of the Emperor of China."

"How delightful!" everyone said. "Now they must sing together. What a duet that will be."

So the two birds sang together, but it was not a success. The trouble was that the nightingale sang in her own way, and the other bird's song came out of a machine. But when the clockwork bird was set to sing alone, it pleased the court quite as much as the real one, for it kept excellent time, and of course it was a great deal prettier to look at, glittering there like a bracelet or a brooch. Over and over, thirty-three times, it sang the same tune, yet it was not in the least bit tired. The courtiers would gladly have heard it a few times more, but now the Emperor thought that the real nightingale should have a turn.

But where was the real nightingale? She had flown out of the open window, away to her own green forest, and no one had noticed.

"Tut, tut," said the Emperor. And the courtiers muttered and frowned. "Still," they added, "we have the better bird here." And the clockwork bird had to sing its song again.

The following Sunday, the Master of the Imperial Music was allowed to give a public display of the bird to the ordinary people. But the poor fisherman, who preferred the real nightingale, said, "It's pretty enough. Yet there's something missing, I don't know what."

The real nightingale was banished from the Emperor's realm. But the artificial bird was awarded a special place on a silk cushion close to the Emperor's bed. It was honoured with the title of High Imperial Minstrel of the Bedside Table, Class One on the Left (for even Emperors have their hearts on the left).

For a whole year the artificial bird went on performing, until the Emperor, his court, and all the Chinese people knew by heart every trill of its song. But one evening, just as the clockwork bird was singing away, and the Emperor was lying in bed, listening, something went SNAP! inside the bird. *Whirr-rr-rr!* The wheels went whizzing round, and the music stopped. The Emperor leapt out of bed and sent for his own doctor. But what was the use of that? So they fetched the watch-maker, and he managed to patch up the bird, after a fashion. But he warned them that it must be used very sparingly; the bearings were almost worn away, and it would be impossible to replace them without ruining the sound.

What a blow! They dared not let the bird sing more than once a year, and even that was taking a risk. However, on these annual occasions the Master of the Imperial Music made a speech full of difficult words saying that the bird was as good as ever. And since he said so, it was just as good as ever.

Five years passed, and a great sorrow fell upon the land: the Emperor was gravely ill, and was not expected to live. Crowds stood outside in the street and asked for news. How was the Emperor? The lord-in-waiting shook his head.

Cold and pale, the Emperor lay in his royal bed. Indeed, the whole court now believed him gone, and went running off to greet his successor.

But the Emperor was not yet dead. Pale and unmoving, he lay in his magnificent bed, with its long velvet curtains and heavy tassels of gold. Through a high open window the moon shone down on the Emperor, and on the artificial bird.

He could hardly breathe. He felt as if something were sitting on his heart. He opened his eyes and saw that it was Death. Death was wearing the Emperor's golden crown; in one hand he held the Imperial golden sword, in the other, the splendid Imperial banner. And out of the folds of the great velvet curtains, strange faces pushed and peeped; some were hideous, others lovely and kind.

They were the Emperor's good and evil deeds, all looking back at him.

"Do you remember...?" "Do you remember...?" came the rustling whispers, one after another. And they recalled so many things that sweat broke out on the Emperor's forehead.

"I never knew... I never realised," cried the Emperor. "Music! Music! Beat the Great Drum of China! Save me from these voices!"

But the voices did not stop. And Death nodded like a mandarin at everything that was said.

"Music! Bring me music!" begged the Emperor. "Beautiful little golden bird, I have given you gold and precious gifts. I hung my golden slipper about your neck with my own hands. Sing, I beseech you, sing!"

But the bird was silent: there was no one to wind it up. And Death went on gazing at the Emperor out of his great empty eye sockets. Everything was still, terribly still.

Then all at once, close by the window, the loveliest song rang out. It came from the living nightingale, who had flown to a branch outside. The little bird had learnt of the Emperor's need, and had come to bring him hope.

As she sang, the ghostly forms grew more and more shadowy, until they thinned away into nothing. The blood began to flow faster through the Emperor's body. Death himself was held in thrall. "Sing on, sing on, little nightingale," said Death.

"Yes, if you will give me the great gold sword. Yes, if you will give me the rich banner. Yes, if you will give me the Emperor's crown."

And Death gave up each of the treasures in return for a song, and the nightingale went on singing. She sang of the quiet churchyard where the white roses grow, where the elderflowers smell so sweetly, where the fresh grass is kept green by the tears of those who mourn. Then Death was filled with a great longing for his garden – and he floated away, out of the window like a cold white mist.

"Thank you, oh thank you," said the Emperor. "You heavenly little bird. I banished you from my realm, and yet you alone came to me in my need, and drove the dreadful phantoms from my bed, and freed my heart from Death. How can I reward you?"

"You *have* rewarded me," said the nightingale. "When I first sang to you, tears came to your eyes, and that gift I cannot forget. Those are jewels that cannot be bought or sold. But now you must sleep. Listen – I will sing to you."

When the Emperor awoke, the sun was shining through the window. He felt restored, all his illness gone. And the nightingale was still there, singing.

"You must stay with me always," said the Emperor, "and sing only when you please."

"No," said the nightingale. "I can't make my home in a palace. But let me come and go as I wish. I shall bring you happiness, but serious thoughts as well. I shall sing of the good and evil that are all around, but have always been hidden from you.

I love your heart more than your crown, yet the crown has some magic about it. Yes, I will come, but there is one thing you must promise."

"Anything!" said the Emperor. "Anything you ask." He had risen from the bed and had put on his imperial robes, and he held the heavy golden sword against his heart.

"The one thing I ask is this: let no one know that you have a little bird for a friend, who tells you everything. Let us keep it a secret."

And with that, the nightingale flew away.

The servants came in to see their dead master. Well – there they stood. "Good morning!" said the Emperor.